The
Little Penguin

by A. J. Wood

illustrated by Stephanie Boey

Dutton Children's Books

New York

Far away in a land where there is only ice and snow, Big Penguin sat, feeling hungry and cold. He looked down at his feet. There, beneath the warm fold of his tummy, was an egg.

His egg.

He had been waiting for it to hatch for a very long time.

"Come on, Little Penguin," he whispered.

Days passed. Suddenly, a noise broke the snowy silence—a CRACK and a peep-peep-peep! Little Penguin had hatched.

"At last," said Big Penguin, looking proudly down at his chick. Little Penguin was covered in tiny soft feathers as gray as the mist that rolled in from the faraway sea.

"One day you will be an Emperor of the Ice like me," his father told him. Little Penguin gazed up at his father and peeped softly.

Big Penguin carried Little Penguin on his feet to a place where many penguins had gathered.

There were Adélies and Chinstraps, Gentoos and Rockhoppers, and great Emperor penguins just like Little Penguin's father.

Little Penguin looked at the big penguins with their sleek, shiny feathers and their long, strong beaks. He wished more than anything for the day when he could look like them.

There were little penguins, too, in a great gray huddle on the ice.

"We will be safe and warm here while you grow stronger," said Big Penguin. "But soon we must set off to meet your mother and swim in the deep waters of the ocean. Stay close, Little Penguin, for it is cold and lonely out on the big ice plain. It is easy to get lost."

But Little Penguin was too excited by the thought of the sea to listen to his father's warning.

At last it was time to begin the journey.

Little Penguin stuck close to his father, but as the day wore on, he began to grow bored. Ahead he spied a great bank of snow with a strange creature sitting on top.

"*I wonder what that is,*" peeped Little Penguin, and he wandered off to take a look.

It was a huge bird, bigger even than Big Penguin.

"And who are you?" snapped the bird.

"I am Little Penguin, and one day I will be an Emperor of the Ice like my father."

"That seems very unlikely," the bird croaked rudely. "Look—your feathers are all falling out!"

Little Penguin looked down in dismay at the clumps of feathers that had fallen to the snow.

He peeped for his father, but there were no penguins in sight. "What do I do now?" cried Little Penguin fearfully. "Which way did they go?"

The strange bird just flapped its great wings and took off into the sky.

Little Penguin started to walk across the snow. With every step, more of his feathers fell around him.

"Soon I will have no feathers left at all," he peeped sadly.

Little Penguin felt as though he had been walking for weeks when he came across a baby seal.

"Who are you?" asked the seal.

"I am Little Penguin, and I am trying to find the faraway sea before all my feathers fall out."

"Then you'd better hurry up," said the seal, "for you will surely freeze once your feathers are all gone."

So Little Penguin walked on, even as night fell. Then he noticed something strange in the distance. It looked like a giant sheet of ice, but it shimmered and rippled in the moonlight. Suddenly, two penguins came hurrying toward him—his mother and father!

"We looked everywhere for you," said his mother, nuzzling Little Penguin with her beak. "Come swim with us in the ocean."

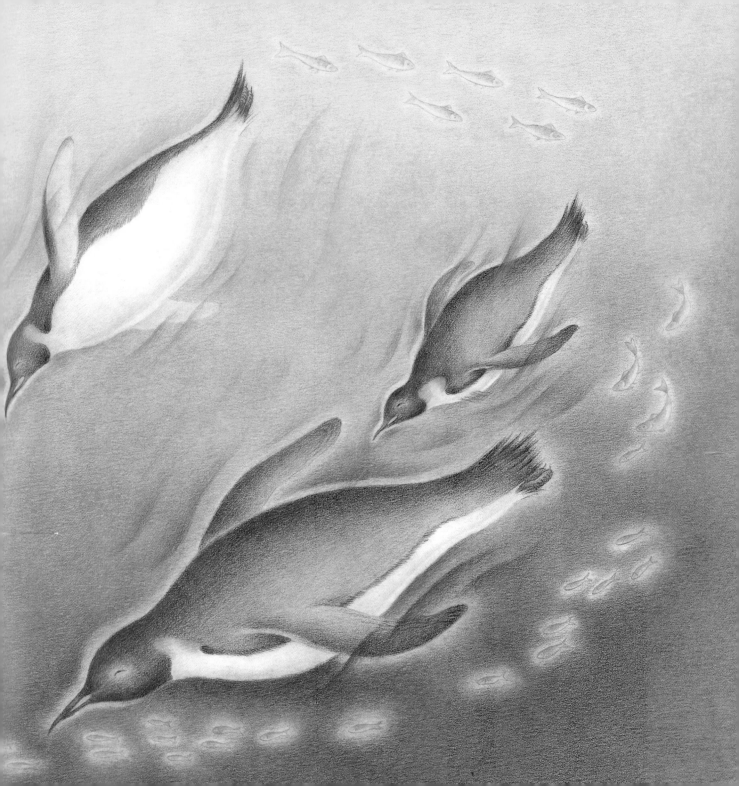

"Won't I freeze without my feathers?" Little Penguin asked his mother nervously when they were sitting back upon the ice.

"But you have beautiful feathers," exclaimed his mother. "Look!"

And when Little Penguin gazed at his reflection in a spot of smooth ice, he saw for himself: his soft gray feathers were gone, but new ones had grown in their place—sleek, shiny feathers, just like his father's.

"Now you, too, are an Emperor of the Ice," said Big Penguin. And Little Penguin felt excited and proud, for at last he knew it was true.